MARINE DRIVE

The sea will never let you create a desire line" Conlon tells us. And so it is in this exhilarating collection of short fictions which pulse with the rhythms of the sea as they shift us through "points of interest" from pier to shore to pavilion roof via starboard buoys, candle smut and heavy steel rings.

Sentences rise and fall, like the pots and pans at sea set into cacophonous motion by a passing tanker, as Conlon deftly, humorously – "up to the church, down to the pub" – navigates the melancholy of faded towns and lost people, the "reckless" play of youth and commuter-carriage lives versus life "on the ocean wave".

In prose redolent of the clear precision of Lydia Davis, the material evocations of Sheila Heti, and the visceral spikes of Ann Quinn, *Marine Drive* speaks brilliantly to the current convergence of ecological, political and social crises in which we are all bodies at sea.

This collection soars!

— Andrea Mason, *Waste Extractions*

Also by Sarah-Clare Conlon

cache-cache (Contraband, 2022)

Sarah-Clare Conlon is an editor and copywriter based in Manchester, where she studied French and, 20 years later, Creative Writing. Shortlisted for the Bridport Prize and a Salt Prizes winner, she has been Best British & Irish Flash Fiction listed. She ran critically acclaimed live literature night Verbose for three years and her prose and poetry is widely published, including by *Cōnfingō*, Dostoyevsky Wannabe, Dunlin Press, *Flash*, *Lighthouse*, *PN Review* and *Stand*. The inaugural Writer-in-Residence at Manchester's Victoria Baths, she co-skippered a Twister around the Irish Sea in 2007 then across the Channel to and through France to the Med.

Marine Drive

Sarah-Clare Conlon

ISBN: 978-1-915079-41-1

Cover designed by Aaron Kent

Edited and typeset by Aaron Kent

Broken Sleep Books   Broken Sleep Books
Rhydwen   Fair View
Talgarreg   St George's Road
Ceredigion   Cornwall
SA44 4HB   PL26 7YH

Contents

For Sue & Clive

Points Of Interest
i. Dovestones

We make for the concrete cornerpost plughole. Whizzing across the water, backwash fizzing, breeze whispering a fresh song off the gritstone tops. Controlled havoc created without warning, we haul in and tack back towards shore. On the pier, waving... trees, sails, flags, hands. It is time, and they are waiting.

ii. Pwll Ceris

We took to sitting on the pavilion roof that summer we looked after the dog, to start with because he had a tendency to nip our ankles; later because of the view. As well as having the ideal vantage point to see the bowling green and shout down the winner of each end, we had a clear sight up the straits and out to sea. On warm nights, once the game was over and the players had packed away their woods, we'd count the starboard buoys casting their emerald glow over the left-hand side of the waters. I'm still counting.

iii. Seine

We didn't repeat what was said in the bar black with graffiti and rock posters and candle smut. It made us reckless. The stolen bottles of beer. The shoes swinging on the wire. The running from alarms. The paranoia about shadows. The weed in the river.

We lay on our backs, heads over the quayside, throats exposed, to see who gave into their stomach first. We walked the planks of barges moored with creaking lines to heavy steel rings that poison hands with the stink of old coins. We played sentry go on Pont Neuf, charging a toll to cross: a poem, a dance, a song, a sword fight.

We chatted the darkness into submission, never mentioning the thing hanging over us, then, as the pooled glass of the highest Left Bank windows coloured orange, we caught the first Métro home, and got on with the rest of our lives.

iv. The Downs

We packed away the remaining fine bone china, strapping it into the scuffed wicker basket. The blackbird became insistent, its clamour piercing the scorched evening air. Tail feathers flicked high, wings hanging beside its flanks; shirt sleeves on an untidy clothesline. Distress call better late than never.

What was it you soothed me with then? Not to worry, it's only a cup – it wasn't a full set to start with. It was once, I sighed.

We'd picked up the hamper on our travels, fashioning the occasion around the purchase, inviting our friends to join us on the heath beneath the water tower, coaxing them out of the safety of their homes and into the unwavering heat. It'll be fun, we said, a proper picnic, like in the good old days. We'll have red salmon sandwiches with cucumber and no crusts, and homemade lemon drizzle, and fizz out of flutes.

We will sit on a tartan blanket.

The ties are looser now, though there was always something missing. This just proved it; the smashing of brittle porcelain on baked ground, the breaking of the silence. Friends come and enemies go. There's always a stock needed sign in the charity shop window.

The General Synopsis At Midday

It has been hallucinations since the Douglas Complex of gas and oil rigs, although the bright blue shooting stars and the puffin outriders port side were real enough. The moon casts shadows, which is unexpected, but not as unforeseen as chimneys blowing smoke in the middle of the sea; these of course exist only in our own imaginations. As the sun comes on watch, the fuzzy mass of the Isle of Man rises from the waves. It seems to be alight, coruscating copper orange licking the edges of the cliffs, a purplish patina appearing above.

I'm at the mast, uncleating the halyard then easing the mainsail down towards me, flaking it first, then strapping it to the boom with white ribbons and Flemish knots, grasping hard myself as the bow muddles through a patch of rough. As we prepare to make landfall, the realisation strikes that we are off course by a number of degrees. The sea will never let you create a desire line – its tides dictate which path you follow despite your best efforts at civil disobedience. We recalibrate our approach and blurs take shape and become solid entities and suddenly there is Mann's capital – its futuristic ferry terminal, its Tower of Refuge ramparts, its red blinking concrete dolphin. Marking the end of the Battery Pier breakwater, this warns unsuspecting mariners of naturally occurring overfalls where currents collide. The devil is in the detail.

It is almost midday on Wednesday, almost 24 hours since we locked out in the shadow of those liver birds, under the watchful eyes of the cardinal buoy cormorants; almost 24 hours since we spoke to anyone other than our crew of two, us. Now, the male voice on Channel 12 tells me we have to wait for the flap-gate to be lowered and the road bridge to be manoeuvred before we can access the pontoons of the marina; our new home, at least for a short while. The window of opportunity is two hours either side of high water, depending on land-based traffic – he is hopeful about getting us through before the lunchtime rush hour. Until then, it's a case of swanning about in the outer harbour, avoiding the Steam Packet, or tying up on Battery's temporary berth.

I fetch fenders and work on persuading my fingers to manipulate their ropes into repeated round turns and two half hitches. It's easier said than done, but the call comes through and we're on, inching our vessel into place, me jumping ship onto the diving board jetty and grappling the sheets onto cleats without stumbling or swearing, making out I've done this before, many times. There's an audience gathered above our heads, absentmindedly picking at paper packets of chips, eyes glued, before dissipating back up the narrow streets away from the slip, back into the bosom of the town. You cut the engine and silence descends, just the slapping of water at the Plimsoll line, the shouting of seagulls bouncing off the high harbour walls.

54° 08.9N, 04° 28.0W

Noon, Tuesday. We're up on Marine Drive, which teemed with tourists in those halcyon days of late Victoria thanks to its groundbreaking electric tramway and engineering feats of ironwork bridge spans at Horse's Leap and Pigeon Stream power house and re-purposed funicular lifts. A crenelated triple-arched toll gate built by the men behind Blackpool Tower guards the entrance to the scenic route, doffing a cap to Llandudno. Both the Pleasure Beach and the Great Orme are 63 miles from here if traditional transportation methods were embarked upon to flee.

Sea side there are sheer drops of layered slate and scree-slathered steep slopes; land side, it's buckled strata exposed to the elements, topped with coastal fields. The wind can be fierce here, and the Manx choughs and wagtails don't hang about. Clinging on for dear life in the hellish cliff-edge gusts is sulphur-coloured gorse and flaming orange Lucifer. Honey-scented heather and burnt-toast bracken squat on the higher tussock mounds and hillsides. These are the fires I caught sight of from my crow's nest. My back is turned to the view expanding outwards from the Camera Obscura across the harbour and lighthouse north towards the Solway Firth. I'm heading south, wondering about the future for the former pleasurelands of Port Soderick, once upon a time all sex-segregated swimming areas, bathing huts, dance halls and fancy eateries. The sky-blue painted paddling pool has filled with pebbles; the fairy glen's guesthouse buildings are dilapidated and derelict, fit only for demolition. Where once there were sea lions in enclosures, now only a sea fret rolls in, trapping me from casting off and heading on to the Holy Island adrift in Welsh waters.

It is July going into August but even so the colour-saturated postcards in salt-rusted metal display racks down on the front don't ring true. Deposited back in Douglas, like the shingle pushed by the tide into Port Soderick's concrete crevices, I leave the Ruabon red station, start and end point of the longest narrow-gauge steam railway in Britain. Across the street lolls the Tongue Building, with its chart-packed chandlery and sump-smelling marina offices; its all-important blue-glossed noticeboard displaying the latest Shipping Forecast and lifting bridge timetable. Calm conditions are promised; an escape is on the horizon. The moment to ready for departure is upon us; we check the radio. The capital's population of 27,938 mill about their business as we wander down to the prom going about ours, dodging clattering horse-drawn trams, another of the island's unique infrastructure solutions. We're off in search of a final fish supper in one of the pubs, still smoky in spite of the recent mainland ban. Our other task is to commit to memory the names of the hotels whose grand bay windows give out onto the Irish Sea: the Empress, the Sefton, the Ascot, the Claremont, the Regency. They'll be useful later for willing on sleep, before the rude awakening to catch the tidal gate lowering when even the sun hasn't given a thought to rising.

Who The Wild Things Are

There were tears in the eyes of the man with curly silver hair as he explained her quirks; how she liked things done, how she responded in certain situations. He wanted to leave her in capable hands. He passed us sugary tea in tin mugs then split pins and shackles and other flotsam and jetsam. When our fingers brushed, we smiled, but ours were smiles of sympathy and his was of sadness.

It was the same when we came to leave. We'd spent months together and weren't sure when we'd see her again. We felt off balance, a hollow ache in our stomachs, a metallic tang in our mouths, but summer was ebbing away and our old life was calling us back in.

She was so beautiful, and we basked in the admiring glances of strangers. When we went out, we were intoxicated. We felt invincible and free, and sat up through the night with only the moon and shooting stars for company. We licked the salt off our lips and swept the hair from our eyes, let loose our hallucinations until the sun rising warmed our bones.

*

A sudden gust propels us into the surging surf, and horses' tails flick up over the bow. The main sail blows taut with a snap and the halyard dings against the mast. My right hand grasps the tiller which pulls excitedly at this speed; my left wipes spume off my face with a diesel-soaked glove.

We cross the wake of a gargantuan tanker and the pots and pans percussion sets to below as we crash through the froth. Three men on the stern wave and we're so close I can see the cigarette butts hanging from their upturned lips.

We avoid bobbing bottles and tin cans, planks of wood. We skirt lobster pots marked with rusty oil drums. Sometimes we dodge even bigger containers, fallen from ships during storms.

We live on the edge, like our neighbours, the trawlermen and riggers. We stuff down snacks because we can't make a square meal and glug rum to keep the sickness at bay. We yell songs into the wind and tell crass jokes and piss over the side and shout at seals and lob crusts at puffins.

It's fierce and unforgiving out here, and we live as savages. It's as well the man with curly silver hair can't see us at times like this.

a blast of light and then it's gone

She goes up to Sparrow Park to clear her head. Always has done. She likes the view since they chopped back some of the trees; the contrast between the industrial skyline and the wild landscape, the hills and the mills. I thought it was a shame, fewer nesting and roosting spots for the songbirds and finches, but she says it gives her more space to think. You can see across roof tiles and factory chimneys and church spires, which I expected would make a free spirit like her feel hemmed in, but she reckons it gives her more perspective.

You can trace where the Silk Road and the railway line criss-cross the river, which veers off to meander along a valley brimming with bulrush-clogged mini oxbows stippling the land's surface, herons watchful at the blurred edges, Constable-esque cattle mooching in the shallows. On days like this, there are two ridges of peaks at the town's border – the real ones with fairytale names like Wildboarclough and Shutlingsloe, and a shadow version where the fuzzy felt clouds sit low in the sky and threaten to smother the town. It never seems to stop raining any more, summer or not.

I worry about her slipping on the wet setts as she takes the steep 108 Steps or Step Hill or Brunswick Hill back to Waters Green, three narrow ribbons unravelling over the sandstone cliff. Up to the church, down to the pub, a physical reminder of a philosophical dilemma, I used to joke, but those drenched cobbles can be lethal. The vertiginous slopes are camouflaged at this time of the evening, too, light creeping only so far from the setting sun and the old Victoriana gas lamps even the moths can barely be bothered batting.

I follow the trail of keen climber jasmine and water-loving flag irises, the petrichor perfume like the damp earth disrupted by copper-sized raindrops. It reminds me of the dripping umbrellas that August as we entered the chapel, feet sodden before we'd even started on the tears. There's the familiar graze of raindrops on my cheek as I peer in at the window, unseen in the dimming dusk. It looks so warm inside, homely, the crimson painted walls above the wooden dado, the green baize of the pool table, the yellowy light from the strips in the kitchen. I imagine the smell of freshly baking plate pies, chips strong with vinegar, top notes of drip trays.

Everything feels unreal, otherworldly, dreamlike. I could have been here for many moons or mere minutes, I can't tell. It's as if I'm floating and might accidentally bump against the glass and draw attention to myself at any moment. Suddenly, there is movement beyond the pane, barely perceptible, but movement all the same. I fix my eyes on the spot where I sensed it, refuse to let my eyes glaze. I spy it again: the flick of a skirt's selvage around the door jamb, the soft satiny thrill of a golden halo of hair.

I remember the two white doves almost kissing on the wing as they flew across the golden box of your favourite Nina Ricci fragrance on the dressing table. You kept it next to the lacquered wooden abalone inlaid jewellery casket some uncle you never met brought back from some war out east for your mother, his sister, back in the Forties. L'Air du Temps, born the same decade and now knocking on seventy years old, is the scent, still going strong with its head of jasmine and heart of gardenias nestled in base notes of sandalwood and iris. The scent of you.

The rain has set in, turning roads to rivers, torrents tumbling along tarmac down to the green where the waters sit still and deep enough for mallard males to stop awhile and show off their shimmering plumage to the mottled hens. Slowly at first and then in droves the fowl gather where the water gathers. It has a colourful history, this basin-shaped dip, important for dyeing in those days gone by when the streets echoed with the looms rattling to the exotic sounds of charmeuse, chiffon, crepe de chine, damask, organza, shantung, taffeta, tussah… the expensive hard-won threads stolen from spinner insects in far-flung places, spies disguised as monks stealing from the stealers. Silkworms sicken easily and are sensitive to atmospheric change. On cold days, fires are lit to warm the air.

Silk was the undoing of me.

You had to make sacrifices to join me here, I know that, which is why I showered you with gifts and whispered sweet nothings. You said the dimly lit flagstoned lanes with their high lichen-tattooed walls penning them in reminded you of the old place, teetering at the crown of the capital. A maze of secret passageways crammed one on top of the other yet fraying at the edges into mossy common and ancient woodland and algae-green pools. You said you didn't mind, that the train was fast and stopped here so often you could nip back whenever you fancied; catch up with your friends, catch up with fashion.

Deep down I worried. I worried your head would be turned again, that you wouldn't step onto the platform where I would wait with sprays of scented freesias and gypsophila baby's breath, wait with my own breath bated, wait with hope in my heart but tears in my eyes. Yet the door would slide open and there you always were, braced for the sudden cold and brandishing like hard-won trophies stiff paper carriers filled with soft pastel tissue cushioning exotic treats and shiny trinkets. With a magic only you seem to possess, you uncovered amazing adornments and precious ornaments where others noticed nothing of value, shelling out little yet looking a million dollars. London was your treasure trove.

I'm still here at the window gazing in, mesmerised as you dance backwards and forwards in the glow from the downlights, reaching, leaning, stretching, bending, as if you're performing on a stage. I'm your audience, rapt. A spider has built a whole home a hair's breadth away from my face since I've been watching you, creating its own version of the fanlights above the grand entrances on the Georgian houses up top. Another spinner like the silkworm; that silk dress I got you for our anniversary as flimsy as cobwebs.

Too much, you said, too much. I thought you meant the pattern, but you'd told me how much you loved the pieces in the visiting exhibition, especially Ossie Clark's trademark brightly coloured plunge dresses. You'd told me he was born in Warrington, not far, and you showed me a postcard of the painting by his best man David Hockney, another Northerner, of Mr and Mrs Clark and Percy. Mrs Clark was a fashion designer from Bury called Celia Birtwell, you said, and Percy was the newlyweds' pet cat when they lived in Notting Hill, in London. I asked if that was the hill you lived on, but you said no, that one's out west, yours was up north, of course. I remembered it all, you were so enthralled, which is why I wanted you to have the dress. When you finally believed me that it hadn't cost the earth and you slipped it on and we went out to celebrate twelve years since tying the knot, I was the one enthralled. I couldn't stop staring at you – and no one else could either.

When you'd told me about the invite to the museum's special launch party with that girl from the paper, I'll admit I'd been a bit crestfallen as I'd wanted to take you out that night, but you came back, as always, and so excited too. Gifts for a beautiful wife are always a bind to come up with, but when I realised twelve years meant silk, I could think of nothing else. It shouldn't be that difficult, I remember thinking, the place is dead most of the time, so I wandered by on my way to and from work every day for a fortnight to see who covered which shifts and who the openers and closers were. The tiny covered buttons were tricky in the subdued light they maintained to protect the fabrics, but I managed, and I got a nice card and some wrapping paper in the gift shop, so at least I gave something back. I definitely have since.

It's gold this year. I've got something for you. I don't know if you'll accept it, but you're still here. You could have got on a train, gone back to London, gone back to those friends and fashions, gone back to that flat in Hampstead overlooking the heath. You could have, but you didn't. You're still here and I still have hope in my heart. I've got your perfume. It's not much, but I know you'll like it. We'll both like it. I take a deep breath and push the door etched Public Bar. We'll see what happens.

Tempered Glass

We meet at the edge of the common, where the road disappears over a lip – the city, the world, spread out below.

You tell me your plan: Clapham, now, Bournville's Valley Pool next, then a heart-shaped lake in Fallowfield. You don't mention Scotland or Wales or Ireland, and I wonder if you lack ambition, or if they lack the facilities. I mistake the streaks on your cheeks for rain as we shelter in the dripping bandstand, me cradling my handbag as if it were a lapdog, you, giant, resting the years-old yacht on your knees.

When umbrellas are shaken dry around us, we plot for the Long Pond, where you plop the model into the water; a concrete-penned miniaturised universe. As you straighten up and wipe your fingers on the herringbone of your jacket, I spy a high-vis tabard making headway towards us, a man shouting. *Membership*, *licences*. You shift your feet, refuse eye contact. His words, and the vessel, veer off; both sentence and sail snagged on a sudden stiff gust.

Our gazes follow the boat's wake across the glass. Billowing canvas is a symbol of adventure and escape, I squeak, grabbing your hand in the excitement – I read it in a book on the Arts and Crafts Movement.

Once the last of the bubbles has broken the mirrored surface, we turn and walk back to the edge of the world. I grab your hand again and peer down. It's all still there, except now it's ours to share.

Surface Tension

She handed me a spare key, said the locksmith would provide one for the front entrance when he came to fix it, then went back to taking money for swims. I pulled the door from the ticket office to, climbed the first couple of steps towards the flat and stopped. Bright colours swam in front of my eyes; a sunset, two swallows, ascending. They only fly low when rain is on the way; you told me. I caught my breath and continued upwards, past the first floor where she'd said the kitchen and sitting room could be found and on to the second, where the beds and baths were.

From 1945, it had been a self-contained four-bed home for the Superintendent, his missus and a couple of kids. Nice nuclear family. The last lot moved out in '72, when the washhouses department was demoted, everyone having inside facilities and all. Turn right out of the door at the top, she'd said, then second on the right, after the tub. It was hot up here, fuggy. The room she'd specified could probably use some modernising, but my granddad had taught me about roses so I didn't mind the flock so much and it had been hung proper; no spaces and plumb straight. It'd do fine.

When I saw her again, the next day, she told me about the lockers. Not many folk used them – nobody nicked clothes, not really, so they were only for valuables, and most people didn't come to the Baths laden down with the crown jewels, she laughed. As swimsuits came pocketless, the keys were looped onto elastic bands you slid over an ankle or wrist. It was up to me to fish out any lost ones, either with the hook that lived in the pool attendant's cubicle, or by going in myself, if I spotted an escapee near the six feet sign, or if its owner pointed it out. They had to wait until the session had finished to be reunited with whatever precious items they had stashed away, as I had to wait until the public were out before I was allowed to get in myself.

Trunks were part of the package. The job had come up on the noticeboard in my last place and the gaffer reckoned I should go for it – being a sailor and all, he'd said, all that water. I thought it might help, too – cleanse the body, cleanse the mind – but now a bit of the old eau-de-vie was all I was thinking about. Drown my sorrows or lift my spirits, whichever way I fancied framing it. Her at the turnstiles had other ideas, though, pushing a cake tin under my nose and telling me to find a knife. It's tradition, she reckoned, to welcome new residents.

On the live-in caretaker's to-do list was making the rounds at the end of each day to collect up any bits and bobs that had been left behind in the nooks and crannies of the hangers and benches in the changing rooms standing sentry around the sides. Goggles, hair bobbles, rubberised caps, metal nose clips, verruca socks, wet flannels, slippery cossies. Most of it ended up in the furnace, helping, in its small way, to heat the amenities. The real treasure was hidden in a wooden box, handmade way-back-when with lovely dovetailed joints, stowed under the ticket booth window, gradually pickling in the smell of chlorine, ready to catch the back of the throat of any light-fingered types.

Men's watches, ladies' earrings, children's sew-on patch badges honourably won for retrieving black bricks or water-logged dolls and swiftly forgotten in the ensuing excitement – all these found themselves under lock and key, in her care. Even the odd wedding ring, rosary beads and, once, she laughed, open-mouthed, a set of false teeth. My daily tasks also included winding the complex system of pulleys and levers activating the greenhouse-style louvered roof windows, pre-unlocking or post-locking-up, opening or closing depending on whether it was first thing or last thing.

*

With the longer days, the sun really warms the place up, and the air becomes so thick with water, you can almost taste it, see steam rising and imagine it working its way into the cracks and crackles of the tiling. Summer is here, but the swallows have yet to return, the real ones at least. Instead I've taken to nodding at the four when I'm fixing or tidying in the Turkish Baths, along with the two in the stairwell that took me by surprise when I first arrived. All six are in pairs – swallows mate for life, I remember you telling me, and, I read in the library, in stained glass like here and in stories, they stand for everlasting love and loyalty. You'd have liked that; I wish you were here so I could tell you. If I could show you, it'd be even better: the way the light flows through the birds' bodies and hits the speckled terrazzo marble floors around the pools, making their own puddles of shimmering colour. It's like looking up at the streaming rose window in a vast dark cathedral then stumbling out into the bright sunshine of a foreign square and not being able to see anything else. Even if you don't believe, it's the kind of thing that changes a man, moves him somehow.

Anyway, her on the front desk caught me mid ritual last week, doffing my cap at the leaded glass. I had to pretend I was being bothered by a fly; swooping my hands about like I was daft and swatting at nothing. I think she's also cottoned on to my other new habit; my early-morning dips. Yesterday, she asked me about a damp towel she'd found lying about, then in the afternoon she brought up tattoos. I wondered if she'd spotted mine – I did catch a flamenco flick of skirt at the door; maybe she was spying on me swimming. I can't resist. I've been here so long now, the pools are part of me, running through my veins instead of blood. The sea feels a long way off – misted over, like the changing-room mirrors.

When the envelope drops onto the mat, I know instantly what it is and put it to one side until later, after my shift. It deserves to be opened along with a new bottle so I can raise a glass to your memory. The swallows will have carried your soul to heaven, so once I've locked up for the evening, I make for the flip-down gallery seats above the Gala Pool with all three things: brandy, glass and letter. I want to be as high up as possible but still bathed in the light from the coloured see-through galleons in full sail, off on adventures, as we had once been. I pour the liquid and hold up the drink to toast them. Lost at sea. In memoriam…

A shadow flashes the length of the pool, a perfect V like the wake of the Olympic hopefuls who practised their butterfly strokes and front crawl here not so many moons ago, in the Baths' heyday. It's only a flicker, a glimpse, and I can't be sure, so I sit stock still and wait, feeling the ghosts of memories creeping up on me, building up inside again. And then it's back, skimming the surface, and my eyes follow its trajectory along the meniscus, not daring to blink, holding my breath, as if I am under the water watching. I feel suddenly elated, reunited with my loss but at the same time relieved, ready to move on at last. The water is calm, not a ripple, but the whole world has changed. There's been a seismic shift yet no one except myself noticed, like when an old pit folds in on itself in the dead of night and only a wonky picture on the wall has a tale to tell.

I grab my three important things and climb down the wooden stairs with the carved, curved banister, down from the balcony to the head of the pool, the deep end. I strip off my shirt and pants, sit on the side and ease myself in. Toes, feet, ankles, calves, knees, thighs, then let go. It's buoyant and warm, or maybe that's the brandy. As I push off, I look up and the woman from the ticket office is gazing at me, smiling, her lips painted red.

I wonder if they were from the start, I just hadn't noticed. I smile back and push forward. It's not long afterwards that I finally take the plunge and have a dagger put through the heart of the swallow that's inked over my heart. I know you're not coming back. I keep the second swallow alive – after all, I'm still here, still swimming, and maybe now I've come to terms with things and you've set me free, I'll be able to find true friendship, maybe even love, once again.

See You Poolside

The heat had been building all summer and, when it broke, the deluge breached the train roof. A party-for-one pastel cocktail-in-a can rode the murky puddle sloshing to and fro with each camber, a carriageful of passengers' eyes following, mouths downturned.

We'd climbed on at Clifton Junction, from the trains-to-the-city platform, our feet already soaked for the second time that day. The stop teetered above the factory where we'd worked in the office, photocopying product manifests from master copies kept in bottle green hanging files in floor-to-ceiling cabinets. First folding then slipping them into punched plastic envelopes, we'd dispatch the makeshift manuals filled with dangerous ingredients and dilution instructions to the sales team holding a lofty court above the bottling belt.

From the station, the sun would catch the river trickling in the valley, glinting, the canal choking on bulrushes and pond skaters, lilypads and dragonflies. Debbie had likely been unaware of either's existence as we'd chatted on the bench beside the manmade pond outside reception, picking at our yellow-stickered sandwiches.

We could be found there most lunches that July, so it didn't take much to fathom whose footprints led to the ladies' from the entrance. Bad timing: management usually took their break later, by which point the floor would have been dry and the chief executive wouldn't have slipped up, and the important clients who'd arrived early would have been none the wiser. Our shoes were back on for when we were given our marching orders, breaking point finally reached.

Warning Signs

We passed starboard of the cardinal, the hazard on our left. Actually, the danger lurked within, dormant. When you upped and left, cadging first a lift then the high-speed train south and across the border, you blamed me for never taking my nose out of my charts and books. In my mind, I was keeping us on track, plotting a successful route through life.

You went off to run a solar farm in the middle of Spain, trading in plans of the wide open big blue for a dry crusty soil in turns rust red and saffron yellow. I heard that you got hitched and got lumbered with umpteen kids, something you always swore you would despise. Sometimes I think you tell people what they want to hear.

Sometimes, I wonder about you in a land you can't call your own, in a ramshackle tumbledown house in the middle of a field in a town overshadowed by a concrete space rocket water tower and a right-wing mayor, graffitied commuter carriages put to sleep in the shade of sidings, containers for freight emptied by bandits in the dead of one hot, sheet-soaked night. I think of you surrounded by your gaggle of a clan speaking words you don't understand behind your back, to your face, and I think of you surrounded by your beloved solar panels: shimmering, pearlescent pools of liquid technology that will never cool you off or quench your thirst.

I heard that you got sacked from the sun plant. Not one, but a good number of the absorbent panes were observed by the powers to be misaligned, pointing away from the fat star, not towards it. That's what happens if you turn to face the wrong direction, I shrugged, and I considered how you might feel about the way things had finished up. Maybe the books and charts weren't so bad, after all. Perhaps it took an Iberian solar farm failure to provide you with enlightenment.

The cardinal buoy, striped the colours of a wasp, had marked the last resting place of a submerged car that wrestled itself free of the barge it was craned on to and off of for the captain's wife's provisioning trips and plunged headlamps first into the river where it was still navigable, downstream from the city where you also jumped ship. These were the details I enjoyed reading in the pilot: landmarks, points of interest, what the warnings signposted, who why where when.

Although you scuppered my hopes for the future with your Spanish trip, I wouldn't let it spoil my dreams of life on the ocean wave. I continued on with the little boat into the lock system: three canals, two rivers and one sea in my sights. I cracked on as far as I could while the weather held, outrunning the expats – retired teachers beelining off to catch *The Archers* on World Service, former naval officers insisting on flying a special ensign to show off their prowess at the helm. Variously, they would tell tales of aircraft carriers and Eurofighters, the perils of keeping goats for pets and maintaining medieval-style kitchen gardens.

I managed to break free and overwintered myself in the confines of the boat's hull, from time to time becoming trapped in ice, like a beetle in amber, her fibreglass and my bones creaking together, waiting for the yawning thaw and stretching of the new season. We were looking forward to adventure. When we lashed onto the pontoon at the confluence, our new lives lay ahead of us, and this time we knew the dangers. We were ready.

From Nowhere

It's suddenly cold. Thirty-odd degrees and it's cold as an eclipse right now. Welcome maybe, in this stupid heat; even the dogs aren't barking. You're pleased someone cares. New teak toe rails. Freshly painted waterline. Polished hull and decks. Running and standing rigging replaced. Serviced winches; serviced sails. The light goes from red to green, the truck moves forward. The boat's shadow makes its way along the main street to the northern perimeter of town, beyond the hinterland, towards infrastructure, networks, civilisation. The café terrace is roasting again. You catch the waiter's eye; he nods. Nobody knows who you are yet everybody knows who you are. You raise your glass to the retreating stern. It's time to move on for everyone.

From a bird's eye view, the masts you hear like ringing bells can only be seen because of the shadows they cast across the scrubby ground, yellowy compacted rutted mud and chippings, grass as parched as straw, scabs of green where clumps of samphire have taken hold, darker more extensive areas of tall reeds bent sideways by the same wind that thins accents and wears down souls. Stretching along the yearly dredged channel linking the sea back to the river, the remnants of industry. A vibrant patchwork of red brick skin on the older warehouses, orange rusted corrugated iron roofs on the defunct factories and packing plants, bright white caravans and awnings, bright black pools of sump oil and discarded diesel, drab slabs of grey gravestones at the fraying edge of the town, sun-bleached signage fallen off long shuttered shops – all criss-crossed with the silver threads of abandoned narrow gauge rail tracks. Pull out further and to the west the fast frantic river burns blue then spreads sparkling tendrils south to the surfline and spit, while northwards the lagoons and levees give way to grapevines and grassland for horses, eventually a road with proper markings, a city with Roman remains and today's tourists. East, and the flaming chimneys of oil refineries light the night sky and haze over the afternoons.

31

Your earliest memory of this place: voracious, ferocious mosquitoes in the deep sea lock, squeezing the little blue yacht into its confines with a hulking cargo ship called LAGUEPE, aggressive yellow and black like the wasp of its name, its bulk slopping the salt and freshwater mix against the stone sides as the level equalised. Next day, bank holiday, the sky filled with the canopies of kite surfers down at the beach; Jean, the taut, tanned man with the noisy pick-up who fixed the seacock, down there with them. Faded flamingos, black bull-friendly egrets, swallows passing through, beetles the size of bumblebees, fighter planes whizzing overhead; flight paths as important here as waterways. Not a cloud in the sky the flaking blue lifting bridge points at momentarily. A stagnant stench is nagging at your nostrils to pay attention as the ponds start to dry up.

"Officers are appealing for help in identifying an unknown person who presented at police headquarters on Sunday afternoon, at 16h00. The woman is described as being white, aged in her mid to late thirties, 1.7m tall, of medium build, with mousy, shoulder length hair. She was dressed in a white t-shirt, dark blue denim shirt, khaki shorts and grey Velcro-fastened canvas pumps. Officers have as yet been unable to communicate with the woman, who appears to be suffering amnesia, perhaps as a result of shock. Details remain sketchy, although detectives say that several witnesses report having seen the woman cross the market square from the church while the flea market was on, and she was also spotted walking towards town along the Plage Napoléon road, between the members-only fishing harbour and the disused Ste. Distribution Produits Afrique facility, at 14h30-15h00. At this stage, the unidentified person is presumed missing, although officers are urging parties with any information, however insignificant it may seem, to contact them. They are also keen to speak to anyone who might be able to provide details that could assist them in tracing the woman's next of kin, so that they may be informed of her whereabouts. A photograph of the woman, issued by police, is published alongside this article."

The first evening you venture out, you go into the place beside the bridge, don't stray far. Art Deco lines and curves harking back to glamorous parties past, the bar of Le Passe-Port is veiled in a fug of smoke emanating from largely Antipodean skippers who run luxury cruisers along the coast. You try not to talk too loudly so they don't try to talk back. This lawless town waits at the edge of the world, its free-for-all motorbike-buzzed crossroads the entertainment on a Saturday night before church next morning, then blinking out into the sun and back to the bar. Confess your sins, remember the dead, genuflect, drink, repeat. The next evening, you try the place next to the old sail stores; Le Mistral. A matronly type in a pinny tied at the waist lugs over a frothy beer to the man beside the jangling slot machine, who whinnies like a horse until he is served. Your head hurts. You ask for icecubes. They never materialise.

In the town, the streets are sandy. Tiny pieces of grit are blown in along the shore road past the boat storage, the bridge and the bars, drifting up against kerbs and bus shelters, getting into eyes and steaming bowls of mussels scraped off the pontoons and jetties and groynes in the dawn hours. Cream concrete cottages and terracotta villas shirk behind gates and bamboo fences, sprawling estates of deck access flats cast a knowing glance back over the town's past life as a thriving harbour, modern multi-coloured apartment complexes overlooking the *port de plaisance* give a glimpse into an optimistic developer's vision for the future. There's a school for small children; after a certain age they go elsewhere. There's one supermarket, catering for a hotchpotch population: those who cannot leave, for if you leave you never come back, and those who leave all the time, and only return to overwinter their boats on the cheap or mothball them indefinitely when funds dwindle. There's the church, the cool of its walls inside and out offering salvation, if nothing else does. On the other side of the main square, there's also the Préfecture police headquarters, set back from the road and up steep shortness-of-breath steps, a double-fronted bright white palace that seems grander than its surroundings and usually echoes with emptiness.

The blood droplets on the marble floor and running in the corridors are quite out of place.

One day when it is too hot to strip varnish, mouth scarved, hands gloved, head covered, you venture further afield, past the marina office with its shrugging Capitaine who feigns ignorance to your complaints yet is happy enough to take your cash. Past the easy-wipe concrete fish stall opposite the hall where the old trade union types meet up and mutter, and where the woman with the black eyes and unseasonably big coat called you a whore then scuttled off whimpering. You find a place with some shade and a breeze, a little off the beaten track, sticky squat white wine glasses with green ribbed stems, a strange kind of trap-racing on the screen mounted to one wall. Three sickly sweet orders in, the cheerful barmaid decides to introduce you to another English-speaking liveaboard, an aristocratic type whose money has run dry enough to not travel but not enough to not drink, now accompanied by a good time gal also with nowhere better to go. People get lost here, can get lost here, he mumbles through a cigarette, more ash than draw. Some people come here to get lost.

"Inquiries are continuing to identify the woman who turned up at the police station last Sunday and we have reason to believe that the investigation has taken a new turn and is now focusing on a crime having possibly been committed. [...] Her clothes and hair were caked in yellow mud, some of it still wet, and crusted with blood; samples have been sent away for analysis. Police say a passerby on the shore road describes seeing a woman coming out of the scrub with 'ripped clothes, scraggy hair, scratched legs and a tear-stained face' at around 14h45. It has emerged that detectives are treating her as a visitor, and it is assumed at this point that she arrived in the area by boat, a sailor's knife being the only property – aside from, we have been told by a source close to the investigation, a Saint Christopher medallion – discovered on her person. A separate source, who approached the newspaper after recognising the woman from the photograph we published earlier in the week, claims to have heard her speaking English, and apparently the authorities are still unable to communicate with the woman, who is either unwilling or unable to talk. Both a mediation expert and a translator are expected to arrive in the days to follow to assist further with the case."

A notice snagged with a single staple to a telegraph pole near where the pizza van pulls up each time day turns to dusk reveals excitement on the way before being torn off by the wind that has become relentless. When the time comes and the trestle tables are unfolded on the blinding gravel glittering in the lea of the church and laden with a hotpotch of naughty knickers and cheap spy thrillers – *A Trap For Calone*, *Ten Centimetres Of Flesh*, *A Girl From Nowhere* – you have forgotten. You are too busy focusing on the scarlet fire hydrant at the side of the long shimmering road, the tarmac softening in the glaring sun, cars careening past. It marks the halfway point between the beach and the boatyards and the backwater haven for fishing vessels, and the market square. A searing pain behind the eyes, pointing dead ahead, the edges of your vision the snow of an untuned TV. Your balance is off. As the cross, anchor and heart precious triad of faith, hope and love come into view, you turn to the building opposite and start to climb.

Ditch

When I can't sleep, I itemise the stuff in my fridge. I have become obsessed with meal-planning, oppressed by leftovers. He works his way around the Marsh, he says, checking off each tank one by one.

He knows them by heart; spent a lot of time down there watching the diggers slash open the fields, the bulldozers gouge the farmland, the machines grub out the ancient hedgerows, pulse the soil, pump water, prime the dredging deposit grounds. It was the year they came to the sixth form common room with its cushioned chairs and the mural painted by that lad everyone said was good at art. I hid in one of the kitchen base units, slid the cupboard door across and peeped through the finger cutout until they left.

When they came back, I was ready. Tell them we went down the Marsh for the birdspotting, he'd said. They tested me; asked me to name the bluetits on the feeder outside the headmaster's office. Tell them we went down the Marsh for other stuff too. I was already showing, so they crossed us off their list. I hardly knew her anyway.

A tanker slices across the Marsh like an ice-breaker, the big ditch hidden. What's that, he points at a flash of lapwings settling on No. 6 Tank, yanking me back to the present. He laughs when I say peewits; hands me more chocolate. It's hard to get up when it's time to go. My jeans are too tight lately. He knows I suspect something, has to keep me sweet. The turbine blades chop the air. The hum of the motorway becomes a roar. The heft of the Holyhead diesel blocks out the sun. The car door clicks shut behind me. One day, I'll get out of here. One day.

Falling More Slowly

No one told me about the gannets. How to plot a course, yes. The brutal effects of wind over tide, yes, the wisdom of maintaining a watch rota, the usefulness of making landfall in daylight hours, yes. Acronyms for pre-ignition system checks, tape recording the Shipping Bulletin in case the kettle whistles mid broadcast just as the announcer embarks on Lundy, Fastnet, Irish Sea... Optimum stowage techniques for ginger biscuits, yes.

All the passage-planning information imbued with importance on terra firma and again on the ocean wave, first impressed in fusty classrooms in water sports centres in landlocked cities, finally enacted under the perfect conditions for encouraging the onset of seasickness in the competent crew being tested for promotion to day skipper: scrunched over a chart table trying to use dividers and chinagraph pencils in the semi-gloom of the cabin below with the bow crashing through the swell, one minute peaking upwards, the next facing downwards, like you over the heads, watching the boil-in-a-bag chicken and rice and strawberry jam sponge pudding ebbing away.

All the information that you recite to get yourself to sleep come twilight, only for it to pop up in your anxiety dreams taunting because you forgot to add or subtract an hour from UTC and now you're about to run aground with your nose pointing straight at one of a hundred slimy-green sea-fouled life-sized cast-iron Antony Gormleys off Mariners Road, Blundellsands.

But no one mentioned the gannets. *Sky-pointing is a ritualised flight intention movement.* My uncle was an ornithologist, a shorebird specialist and seabird expert, and one of the country's ringing pioneers at a time when little was known about the precise destination of our feathered friends leaving British shores. Precise destinations, leaving

British shores; this is the currency sailors deal in. The first foreign recovery of one of Uncle John's ringed birds was by an Eskimo in Greenland. The Inuit had shot it down. Subsistence hunting.

Rounding Anglesey, we cross the mouth of the Menai Strait, where a trawler, lights blasting, ploughed right at us one night we cautiously navigated the narrow channel in search of a vacant mooring buoy to snag, grappling its slippery rope onto our cleat. Now, we pass without incident, Puffin Island off to starboard, then Great Orme Head with its clunky cable-hauled tramcars, and radio fame as a star of Inshore Waters. Round this point and the sails fill and propel us across the expanse of Penrhyn Bay, streetlamps stretched along the faded resorts' fronts, linking Colwyn to Llandudno to Rhyl to Prestatyn like an uncoiled string of fairylights. Past Talacre's golden dunes and red-capped Point of Ayr lighthouse, otherwise all white to aid identification against the dark marram grass and gorse and horsetails, and disused since the 1840s, haunted by a man with a broken heart; past the rusting hulk of the Duke of Lancaster passenger steamer last purposefully afloat forty years ago. Here the Dee spills out, all salty silt and sandbanks.

The tilt of the boat is sudden and disconcerting; the jib collapses and flip-flops uselessly. A change in wind direction above and water currents below disrupts our flow and throws us off course, but with a few turns of the winch and some robust tiller action, recovery is swift. Localised gusts and poor visibility was predicted. *East or South East 3 to 5, rain or thundery showers later, moderate or good, occasionally poor, until later.* Grabbing the binoculars, I check the position of our stanchions in line with the next landmark, make adjustments to our coordinates. Still no one has said anything about the gannets. *'Wing busking' is performed as part of the wing movement involved in taking flight. The neck is stretched vertically to its fullest extent and held stiffly, whilst the bill points skywards and the eyes look binocularly forwards.*

I look binocularly forwards. Visibility remains good. Dead ahead squat the three tidal islands at the entrance to the estuary, the border between England and Wales: Little Eye, Middle Eye and Hilbre Island. If I could come to a standstill, I would. I would down tools, stop all the clocks, silence the pianos, sling the hook, clamber over the side, shimmy down the anchor chain and wade through spume and mudflats and rockpools, then crest the sandstone outcrop and lie down in the thrift and bracken, vetch and campions, the only mammal other than the breeding field voles, and the fallow deer, thought to have swum the river to the peninsula.

But we're on a schedule, the wrecks on the chart stark reminders that the tide tables and almanac are there for a reason. All I can do is sit tight and observe the rough water on the rocks to the north of the now-uninhabited Wirral archipelago, observe the collection of cottages making up the Hilbre Island Bird Observatory, where you would sit for hours, days, months, years from 1957, recording, tagging, observing. I observe through the binoculars and I observe someone observing back. It's not you, but maybe it's someone somehow connected to you. *Weather reports from coastal stations, Liverpool-Crosby, South East 2, 27 miles, 1018, rising more slowly.*

On high spring tides in storm conditions, the islands can be carpeted with waders, most commonly knot, dunlin, redshank, turnstone, sanderling, oystercatcher and the purple sandpiper, one of your favourites. The gannets aren't here, of course – they stay further out, away from people, flying parallel to the boat only when the engine is cut, sleek shaped slick shaded with golden highlights and black eyeliner. Very distracting, no one warns you. *There is a tendency for most arrivals to occur between dawn and mid-day, representing birds which departed late the previous day, fished in the early hours then returned.* It is 09.20 when we log the Queen's Channel Buoy, a full three hours later when we lock in from the Mersey.

Let's Go Round Again

1. 200

The canal's tinge is grey suds and the level is too high, but these things are not our concern. Come out from the overhanging canopy still dripping the remnants of a shower into the lapping water, and creamy chippings glare, the sky the bright but dark blue of high summer. A storm has come and gone, not even a black smudge at the edge of memory. Our location is undisclosed, while the lush deciduous woodland gives way to something harder, more concrete; pavements, roads, walls, houses perhaps, workshops maybe. A child's moon peers down, yet the sun is everywhere, and everything is painted as if to blind or at least to stun. The man on the train spoke French, or Spanish; either way, a language dripping warmth and confidences. As we perched on high stools at the counter of the dining car, he leant in and whispered to his colleagues to pass their cups, which he filled from a tall silver coffee pot, the liquid turning to blood red wine on contact with the fine bone china. He smiled at us, teeth as gleaming as his uniform. Hands above his head gently fluttered as the battery fizzled out around one.

2. 150

When we awoke some hours later and descended the steps to the stones beside the railway at the top of a steep bank leading down to a dense copse of trees and a forest floor that released heat from the moss around our ankles and a recollection of psalms some Sunday long forgotten, we realised that we were at a loss to explain how or why we were here. My watch appeared to have stopped at two, whenever that was. Our sneezes disturbed the dormant undergrowth and first a rabbit appeared, then a gamebird the likes of which we had never seen: a ptarmigan, a capercaillie; who knows. The rabbit rubbed its eyes in the white light and the bird yawned and stretched, then both rustled away from us, towards roofs reflecting the silvered surface of an overfilled channel of water, sides slopping as if a vessel had recently passed.

3. 100

Standing, sentry, a heron, one weary bead surveying our approach, the other reflecting the starlight up high, as those very same heavens opened and the leaves of the ancient oaks and rowans and birch and beech reached tipping point and drizzled their moisture onto us and the truffling wild beasts. A cat appearing then disappearing pointed to the source of a desire line traipsing from the trees to the makings of a town, or rather a village, with rattlings from the other side indicating the disturbance of sleepers. A church chimed three, petering out before we reached the path's culmination.

4. 50

The saltpetre flare of the whitewashed brickwork made it impossible to look at, impassable at this time of day, or night. A clock struck four, carriages trundled along, a boat puttered, we sought shelter beneath trees from a sudden downpour. Without the correct codes, we would need to come back.

5.0

Acknowledgements

Thanks to Ella Johnston and Martin Bewick at Dunlin Press for publishing 'The General Synopsis At Midday' in the *Port* anthology, to Helen Rye and Christopher Allen for selecting 'Warning Signs' for publication in the flash fiction special, issue 20, of *Lighthouse Journal*, and to Sally Barrett for publishing 'Let's Go Round Again' in *Mid Life Crisis: The Alice One*. Thanks to Steve Campbell for publishing a version of 'Who The Wild Things Are' as 'The Wild' in *Ellipsis* and to Adam Trodd, Nuala O'Connor and team for including 'The Lookout', a much shorter version of 'Falling More Slowly', in *Splonk*. Thanks to Jude Higgins for publishing an earlier version of 'iii. Seine' as 'Are You Afraid Of The Dark?' in the Bath Flash Fiction Award anthology *To Carry Her Home* and an earlier version of 'iv. The Downs' as 'Inside Out' in the anthology *Flash Fiction Festival Two*.

'Surface Tension' was my contribution, as the inaugural Writer-in-Residence of Victoria Baths, to the Re/Place event for the 2019 Weekend of Words festival. 'Falling More Slowly' was a commission for FaxFiction, an event at Refract:19 festival at Waterside Arts. It was written partly in memory of John Gittins, 'Birdman of Hilbre Island', 8 August 1928–9 December 2001, and quotes The Shipping Forecast issued at 0015 on Sunday 23 June 2019 as well as JB Nelson's 1965 work 'The Behaviour Of The Gannet'. 'a blast of light and then it's gone' was a commission for the Macc Stories project, part of LIT Fest 2019.

Finally, thanks to David Gaffney for a decade of support and encouragement, writing wise, and for his love and friendship, love and friendship wise.

LAY OUT YOUR UNREST

www.ingramcontent.com/pod-product-compliance
Lightning Source LLC
Chambersburg PA
CBHW020812130626
46554CB00006B/2399